Jingle Bells

A New Story by Kathleen N. Daly

BASED ON THE TRADITIONAL

CHRISTMAS CAROL

Pictures by
J. P. MILLER

GOLDEN PRESS
Western Publishing Company, Inc.
Racine, Wisconsin

Ninth Printing, 1978

Dashing through the snow comes the Bear family,
in a one-horse open sleigh. There's Papa Bear and
Mama Bear and two Baby Bears.

"O'er the fields we go!" shouts Papa Bear, cracking his whip. And the sleigh glides down over the snowy fields.

Laughing all the way, the Baby Bears sing Christmas carols and nibble on cold plum pudding.

Hubert Horse loves to pull the sleigh. He flicks his
bob-tail merrily and the Baby Bears sing,
"Bells on bob-tail ring,
Making spirits bright!"
And dashing along they go.

Now they're in Rabbit Warren, a cozy little town, and the rabbits and their friends come out to say, "Hello!"

"Come aboard," says Papa Bear, "we're going for a ride." And Cuddly Bunny and three bunny sisters hop onto the sleigh.

Patrick Pig and his friend Katie Kitten hop in.
Then come Denis Dog and Stewart Seal and Richard
Raccoon.

"What fun it is to ride and sing a sleighing song tonight!" says Esmeralda Ostrich, and she, too, hops aboard and starts singing.

She does not sing very well, but nobody minds because it is Christmas.

Jingle bells, jingle bells, jingle all the way. Oh
what fun it is to ride in a one-horse open sleigh!
That's the sleighing song they sing.

O'er the fields they go, wrapped up in their furs.
All of a sudden,
"Stop!" says a voice.
Who can it be?

It's a man in a red suit and a white beard and big black boots and a sack over his shoulder—it's Santa Claus!

"Help!" says Santa Claus. "I have no six-reindeer open sleigh this year, and I'm too tired to walk any more!"

"What happened?" asks Papa Bear.

"My reindeers all caught cold, and their mother has put them to bed — "

"With bed socks and tea, I hope?" says Mama Bear.

"Yes," says Santa gloomily.

"Well, hop aboard, there's plenty of room," says Papa
Bear.

And Santa hops aboard, sack and all.

Soon he is merrily singing the sleighing song:

Oh what fun it is to ride
In a one-horse open sleigh!
   And so for the first time Santa makes
all his visits in a one-horse open sleigh.
   He brings Tommy a toy train,
and Dora gets a doll.

Rupert gets a rocking horse, and Bruce gets a boat.

When Santa's sack is empty, Santa and his helpers climb
into the sleigh, and Papa Bear cracks his whip, and off
they go, to take Santa home.

And when they get to Santa's house, what a lovely surprise is waiting for them!

Mrs. Santa has cooked a Christmas dinner, with lots

of turkey and plum pudding and special fish for Stewart Seal and Katie Kitten, and crunchy carrots for the rabbits, and juicy corn for Patrick.

After dinner they gather around the biggest Christmas
tree you ever saw.

There are presents for all, and then there are balloons
to blow and games to play—my, what a party!

Before they leave, they peek in at the six little reindeer, all tucked up in bed and sniffling.

"Merry Christmas!" they call.

And the reindeers call, "Berry Christmas!"

Then they all pile into the sled—Papa Bear and Mama Bear and two Baby Bears, Cuddly Bunny and his three bunny sisters, Patrick Pig and Katie Kitten, Denis Dog and Stewart Seal and Richard Raccoon, and Esmeralda Ostrich.

Papa Bear cracks his whip and off they go, in their one-horse open sleigh. And do you know the song they sing?

Jingle Bells!

Dash-ing through the snow, In a one-horse o-pen sleigh,

O'er the fields we go, Laugh-ing all the way;

Bells on bob-tail ring, Mak-ing spir-its bright; What

fun it is to ride and sing A sleigh-ing song to-night!

Jin-gle bells! Jin-gle bells! Jin-gle all the way!

Oh what fun it is to ride In a one-horse o-pen sleigh, Oh

Jin-gle bells! Jin-gle bells! Jin-gle all the way!

Oh what fun it is to ride In a one-horse o-pen sleigh! Hey!